D1360733

SUKI
Silver Anniversary Edition

Suki and the Invisible Peacock
Suki and the Old Umbrella
Suki and the Magic Sand Dollar
Suki and the Wonder Star

Also by Joyce Blackburn

Sir Wilfred Grenfell: Doctor and Explorer

Theodore Roosevelt: Statesman and Naturalist

John Adams: Farmer from Braintree; Champion of Independence

Martha Berry: A Woman of Courageous Spirit and Bold Dreams

James Edward Oglethorpe

George Wythe of Williamsburg: Teacher of Jefferson and Signer of the Declaration of Independence

The Earth Is the Lord's?

Roads to Reality

A Book of Praises

The Bloody Summer of 1742: A Colonial Boy's Journal

Phoebe's Secret Diary: Daily Life and First Romance of a Colonial Girl, 1742

SUKI

and the Wonder Star

SUKI

Silver Anniversary Edition

Suki and the Invisible Peacock

Suki and the Old Umbrella

Suki and the Magic Sand Dollar

Suki and the Wonder Star

Also by Joyce Blackburn

Sir Wilfred Grenfell: Doctor and Explorer

Theodore Roosevelt: Statesman and Naturalist

John Adams: Farmer from Braintree; Champion of Independence

Martha Berry: A Woman of Courageous Spirit and Bold Dreams

James Edward Oglethorpe

George Wythe of Williamsburg: Teacher of Jefferson and Signer of the Declaration of Independence

The Earth Is the Lord's?

Roads to Reality

A Book of Praises

The Bloody Summer of 1742: A Colonial Boy's Journal

Phoebe's Secret Diary: Daily Life and First Romance of a Colonial Girl, 1742

JOYCE BLACKBURN

SUKI

and the Wonder Star

SILVER ANNIVERSARY EDITION

Illustrations by Stephanie Clayton

PROVIDENCE HOUSE PUBLISHERS
Franklin, Tennessee

First edition 1971. Second edition 1996
Printed in the United States of America

00 99 98 97 96 5 4 3 2 1

Library of Congress Cataloging-in-Publication Data

Blackburn, Joyce.
Suki and the wonder star / Joyce Blackburn ; illustrations by Stephanie Clayton. — 2nd ed.
p. cm.
Summary: After visiting Chicago's Adler Planetarium, Suki dreams about the Star of Bethlehem and makes an important discovery about the new boy she thinks is a show-off.
ISBN 1-881576-72-8
[1. Friendship—Fiction. 2. Stars—Fiction. 3. Christmas—Fiction. 4. Japanese Americans—Fiction. 5. Hispanic Americans—Fiction.]
I. Clayton, Stephanie, ill. II. Title.
PZ7.B53223Sun 1996
[Fic]—dc20

96–14845
CIP
AC

Cover design by Schwalb Creative Communications Inc.

Accurate scientific information and helpful suggestions for its use in the original manuscript were supplied by Lee W. Simon and the staff of the Adler Planetarium, Chicago, Illinois.

PROVIDENCE HOUSE PUBLISHERS
238 Seaboard Lane • Franklin, Tennessee 37067 • 800-321-5692

For Stephie, artist, who recklessly abandoned herself to our adventure from the start

1

Every exhibit at Chicago's Adler Planetarium was crowded. The lower hall echoed with voices and footsteps, but no one noticed Suki near the meteorite display counting her money.

So far I've spent fifty-five cents, she figured. *Twenty cents for the bus . . . thirty-five cents for admission to the planetarium.*

One by one, she dropped three nickels, three dimes, and two quarters into her purse and zipped it closed. Out of the dollar and a half saved for today, Suki had ninety-five cents left.

It doesn't cost anything to get weighed, she thought, stepping onto a scale that looked like an old-fashioned lollipop.

A big red arrow swung around and stopped. *If I were on the moon, I'd weigh twelve pounds!*

She hopped off that scale onto the one next to it. (They were exactly alike.) Again the arrow swung around. *On the planet Mars, I would weigh twenty-eight pounds!*

There were three more scales, and Suki tried them all. *On Jupiter, I would weigh one hundred and ninety-three pounds! And on Venus, I would weigh sixty-six! If I were on the sun, I would weigh two thousand and thirty-seven!*

She always weighed on the lollipop scales when she went to the Adler Planetarium for the Sky Show.

It's almost time for the show to start, she realized, checking her wristwatch. *If Butch and Manuel don't hurry, they'll miss the beginning. Manuel is late for everything. When we come alone, Butch stays with me. Manuel comes with us and off they go to the optical shop. I'm glad I said no when they asked me to go too. Who wants to watch kids grind and grind on those mirrors they make for their old telescopes? Manuel thinks he knows everything about telescopes—just everything!*

METEORITES

Oh, well—if Butch wants to be late because of that big show-off, who cares?

Butch was the one person Suki's parents trusted to take her on the bus and subway to museums and concerts and the Cubs' baseball park. There were lots of fun places in Chicago. Suki and Butch were always going somewhere until Manuel had moved next door to Butch. Now Butch acted as though he couldn't take a step without him. Even Suki's sisters tried to get Manuel's attention.

How did that big show-off keep Mari and Yuri and Butch fooled? Spouting long scientific words and Spanish phrases! Always being late and saying, "Ees better to be late than to stay home, *sí*?" Another thing—Manuel laughed all the time. Suki got tired of that and the way he bragged on himself. When he hit a home run, he applauded himself around the bases. When he shot a basket, he crowed, "Beeg Boy do eet with one hand. Watch!" Sure enough, the ball would drop right in again, and all the kids whistled and yelled as though Manuel were a superstar.

Ugh! She couldn't stand him.

After waiting five more minutes, Suki started up the steps leading to the main floor of the planetarium where the Sky Theater was. Lots of girls and boys, grown-ups too, were headed that way this Saturday. If Butch and Manuel didn't come on, there might not be any empty seats.

Thick blue carpet swallowed the crowd sounds inside the theater where seats were arranged in tiers, the way they are in stadiums. Overhead, the white domed ceiling made Suki imagine she was inside a giant eggshell. Once Butch had asked the lecturer to show them the control panel on the opposite side of the theater. Shaped like a horseshoe, it reminded Suki of a plane cockpit with its dozens of switches and dials which guided the great Zeiss projector in the center of the room.

The Zeiss was over seventeen feet long and very heavy. Small projectors were inside the two globes on either end of it. Through porthole-type openings in the globes, pictures of the heavens and star fields were cast onto the domed screen. Butch said the Zeiss projector had forty thousand parts. When Suki asked him how he knew, he replied, "Manuel said so." How tired she was of hearing over and over, "Manuel said so."

Where were those two anyway? As if in answer to her silent question, Butch and Manuel came leaping down the aisle to the row where Suki was seated, squeezed past the other people, and plopped down in the seats next to her.

"Guess what, Suki?"

"What, Butch?"

"We've been watching stuff in the Figuring Room."

"Figuring Room? You mean they have a special room to do their math in?" Suki was being sarcastic, but Butch did not catch on.

"No, dummy, it's where they test the surfaces of their telescope mirrors after they polish 'em."

"A mirror has to be shaped to a fraction of a wave length of light," Manuel said. "Approximately twenty-five ten-millionths (.0000025) of an inch!"

"Oh, I knew that," Suki said. "Now shut up. The music is starting."

If Mother heard me say shut up, I'd be in real trouble, Suki thought, but at the moment, saying it was strangely satisfying.

Gradually, the inside of the eggshell dome changed into the nighttime sky . . . stars and nebulae, planets and constellations were projected onto the almost black space . . . some bright and constant, some faint and fuzzy.

Suki had come to the Adler Planetarium for the Sky Shows ever since she was old enough to sit still. Just the same, when the Zeiss projector whirred into operation, she felt a thrill as though it was her first time. True, her body stayed in the tilt-back chair with its comfortable round headrest, but her mind—her imagination—would ride on the projector's beams out . . . out . . . out . . . light-years away from earth . . . so far that when the lecturer spoke, Suki jumped. The sound of a human voice surprised her.

3

The lecturer began: "Every December astronomers are asked, 'What was the Star of Bethlehem?' And every December we show you how the heavens looked in that part of the world where the Wise Men saw the star almost two thousand years ago."

Suki recognized the Big Dipper, naturally . . . the Milky Way . . . Pegasus. . . . There was the fainter Y-shaped grouping of Pisces. There was Jupiter, and there was Saturn with its rings.

"These stars we are showing you now were like familiar friends to the Wise Men," the lecturer continued. "From their observations of the heavens, these men, also known as Magi, made wondrous predictions and interpreted events. They were probably priests of an ancient religion. The Star of Bethlehem and the Magi are mentioned in only one of the biblical stories about the birth of Christ. In Matthew's gospel we read:

> After Jesus was born in Bethlehem in Judea, during the time of King Herod, Magi from the east came to Jerusalem and asked, "Where is the one who has been born king of the Jews? We saw his star in the east and have come to worship him."

Suki knew the story almost word for word—Daddy read it aloud every Christmas. She never had liked old Herod because of the way he tried to trick the Wise Men into telling him what they found out about the little king, all the time pretending he too wanted to worship Jesus. The truth was that Herod wanted to get rid of anyone who might take over his kingdom. The Wise Men should have guessed that. Anyway, when they left old Herod, the star which had led them such a long,

long way went on ahead, till it came to where the little king was.

The lecturer quoted the gospel story again:

> When they saw the star, they were overjoyed. On coming to the house, they saw the child with his mother Mary, and they bowed down and worshiped him. Then they opened their treasures and presented him with gifts of gold and of incense and of myrrh.

Then the lecturer told how the Magi had decided to make that hazardous, eight-hundred-mile journey from Persia to Jerusalem. Suki had not known before that a camel caravan travels only two and a half miles an hour. It must have taken the Magi a couple of months to make the trip!

"The star was probably a sign for which they had been waiting," the lecturer said. "Being well

educated, they knew the predictions of the Hebrew prophets. One in particular, the prophet Isaiah, had claimed that a perfect king would be born who would grow up and establish a kingdom of peace. The Wise Men must have thought their star was leading them to this promised king. And so they traveled, studying the heavens from night to night, day to day. Shooting stars, meteor showers, and comets were not strange to them. There may even have been *novae*, or new stars, for them to watch. Novae are really old, but some sort of explosion blows off their outer layers, making them thousands of times brighter for a few days or weeks before they fade. There also could have been a meeting of Jupiter and Saturn. Certainly that would have made a great light in the heavens, and what would have been brighter still, there could have been the very rare and spectacular meeting of Jupiter and Saturn *and* Mars. Such a phenomenon could surely have guided them on their long journey."

By now, Suki had forgotten the switches and dials that made moons and suns and planets rise on the planetarium dome. A thin crescent moon appeared on the horizon and there was her favorite, Venus.

"Observe Venus, the brightest." The lecturer used a pointer. "Here, close to Venus was Jupiter, known to the Magi as King of the Gods. And here was Saturn, known as Protector of the Jews. The three planets were meeting, combining their great light. Was this what the Magi saw? Perhaps. We can't be sure, but does it really matter? Couldn't the Star of Bethlehem have been hung in the east just for the Wise Men—a miracle star, a star about which we can still wonder?"

Of course, Suki said to herself . . . *of course, it could have been a star hung in the eastern sky just for the Magi. Astronomers don't need to explain it. Hadn't it led right to the little king just as the Wise Men were certain it would? They gave Him the gifts brought all the way from their homeland, and they worshiped Him. Wasn't that the point of the story?*

Soft music filtered into the background. The lecturer was telling how afterward in a dream the Magi were warned not to go back to Herod. If they had paid no attention to the dream, the story would have ended tragically. Herod would have tracked down the little king and killed Him.

Suki was always relieved that the story did not end that way. She liked the happy ending: the Wise Men went back home without telling old Herod their secret. He never found the little king.

"When you place a star on the tip of your tree this Christmas," the lecturer concluded, "let it be a symbol of the star that guided the Magi to the little king—the little king who grew up and lived here to bring peace on earth, good will toward men."

The sun began coming up, brighter and brighter; the music rose in a crescendo. The Sky Show was ended.

When the theater lights came on, Butch poked Suki and Manuel. "If we hurry, we can get ahead of the crowd. Come on."

Suki hated to have her mood shattered, but she yanked on her coat and followed the boys out of the Sky Theater, past the turnstiles and glass booth at the entrance, through the high brass-framed doors of the Adler Planetarium.

It was snowing again.

4

The bus ride home to the North Side seemed to take forever. Fresh snow made the streets slippery. Traffic slowed, tangled at every corner. Once the bus skidded to a stop, throwing Butch and Manuel hard against Suki, who was squeezed into the corner of the long back seat.

"Don't touch me, you Latin creep," Suki said in a loud voice. The riders who heard her stared at Manuel and snickered. He laughed, but he was blushing.

Butch said, "Aw, Suki, quit actin' like you're gonna break. You know we couldn't help bumpin' you."

Furious, Suki glared out the window. As usual they had left her out of the conversation. *Yak, yak,*

yak—on and on and on about building telescopes. "Newtonian reflecting telescopes," Manuel called them. Boy, did he ever think he knew all there was to know about telescopes! Who cared whether you "rough ground" or "fine ground" a telescope mirror?

"The stuff they polish mirrors with is *barnesite.*" Manuel tossed that off as though he were telling time. He and Butch thought they were junior Einsteins! They were geniuses all right when it came to making her feel stupid and left out. *But wait till we get off the bus at Goshorn's,* Suki thought spitefully. *We'll see who feels left out. Just wait.*

Two doors north of the Gosho Gift Shop, owned by Suki's father, was Goshorn's Delicatessen. It was a hangout for the neighborhood kids, a place where they stopped after school. Goshorn's was crowded on Saturdays, too, from noon till ten o'clock closing time.

Although Suki knew some of the girls standing in line at the cash register, she barely spoke, marching straight past them to the third booth on the right. Fortunately, it was empty. She sat in the middle of one bench so that Butch and Manuel would have to sit on the opposite side, across from her.

Besides all the good takeout salads and meats Miss Goshorn prepared, she was famous for her pastries. Her niece, known to the customers as "the Captain," made fancy sundaes and sodas. Of course, for the old folk who sat at the tiny tables for two, the Captain made hot spiced tea, which she served in thick amber glasses with handles.

Every Saturday, Suki and Butch went to Goshorn's, and every Saturday they had the same things: a chocolate eclair for Suki, a double root beer soda for Butch.

"What're you gettin', Manuel?" Butch asked.

"Notheeng." Manuel shrugged his shoulders.

He never has any spending money, Suki thought, *so why does he always have to tag along? Why in the world doesn't he just go on home?*

After hanging up her coat, she went over to the pastry case to select an eclair. Suki always looked for the one with the thickest icing on top and the most custard inside.

"I'll have that one, please." She pointed out an eclair which Miss Goshorn picked up with some wooden tongs and slipped onto a pink paper plate.

As usual, the Captain was fizzing Butch's soda before he could even order, and, as usual, Butch spilled some of it on his way back to the booth.

"I brought you a straw, too, in case you want some," he said to Manuel. "Or maybe you'd rather have a bite of Suki's eclair." Suki pretended not to hear.

"Suki needs it all for herself," Manuel teased. "It weel make her strong. I am strong already. Feel." He flexed his muscle and Butch pinched the hard bulge above Manuel's bony elbow.

Boys are such dopes, Suki thought. "Aren't you going to try your soda, Butch?"

"Sure, Suki." He took a big noisy slurp. "Wanna trade?"

They always did that. She sampled his soda, he

took a bite of her eclair. But today she said, "No, I like mine better." Then instead of making it last, she hurried to finish the pastry and went right back to the case for another one.

"*Estoy muy triste* [I am very sad]. I don't theenk she likes me," Manuel said.

"Aw, don't let her bug ya." Butch took another loud draw on his soda. "You know, we never took anyone with us to the Sky Show before. She's jealous, that's all."

"Girls!" Manuel wrinkled his nose.

"If she doesn't look out, I won't take her anywhere. I'll go around with you—just you," Butch said. "Say, have you ever been to the planetarium in the summer?"

"Sure, why?"

"Have you seen the giant stars then?"

"You mean like Arcturus?"

"Well, that's one," Butch was saying when Suki returned to her seat in the booth.

"Arcturus has a surface temperature of over eight thousand degrees," Manuel said. "Did you know that, Butch? It's about thirty times as beeg as the sun and geevs off one hundred times more light."

Showing off again, Suki thought, as she scooted back into her place. "I'll bet you don't even know how much light the sun gives off," she said, taking a bite of her second eclair. Custard squished from the corners of her mouth.

Manuel looked at the eclair hungrily but went right on explaining, "The sun geevs off energy per square yard equal to seventy thousand horsepower. If you then multiply all that by the total square yards on the sun—its diameter is eight hundred sixty-four thousand miles—you'll find out how much energy the sun geevs off."

She hadn't meant to give him an excuse to go into all those statistics! "So, how much does that make?"

"More than you or I or Butch or anyone else can figure," Manuel said. He sat there in deep, deep thought while Butch finished his soda.

"Why don't you have another one, Butch?" Suki asked.

"I'm broke, that's why."

"I'll divide an eclair with you."

"What eclair? You gobbled that second one faster than the first!"

Suki was not listening to Butch as she left the booth again.

"She's nuts!" Butch shook his head. "She never has three. I hope she doesn't get sick."

"And throw up," Manuel said.

At the pastry counter, Miss Goshorn looked over the top of her glasses at Suki when she handed her chocolate eclair number three. "If you turn into custard, don't blame Goshorn's!"

Suki didn't really want that third eclair at all,

which made it easier to offer half of it to Butch. Instead of stuffing it right into his mouth, Butch handed it to Manuel. "You take a bite," he urged.

Manuel pretended indifference. "No, I do not eat sweets. Sweets are for leetle children."

"What a *beeg* liar!" Suki said as she squashed the rest of the eclair all over Manuel's face. Then she grabbed her coat, threw some money on the table, and flounced out of Goshorn's.

5

Humming along with the bass notes her left hand played, Suki tried the ending of the piece again and sustained the final chord with the pedal. The piano strings reverberated magnificently.

Most of my pieces are too simple, too delicate sounding, she thought. This Bach arrangement had lots of bass notes that stretched her left hand, and it got louder all the way to the last majestic measure.

"You do very well with that, Suki," Mother said, walking through the family room. *She must have been listening,* Suki realized. *This is the second time she has come in since I began to practice.*

"I love the ending, Mother." Suki said and then she repeated the last three chords.

"Rather loud, though," Mother said, smiling. "I'm sure the customers downstairs think so."

On Saturday nights, Daddy kept the gift shop open. Usually, Suki did not practice on Saturdays; that was *off* day. Once her room was cleaned and the bed linens changed, she could do as she pleased. But tomorrow night was the contest program at the Koinonia Koffee House. Over twenty kids in the neighborhood would be in the contest. Her sisters would play their twangy guitars and sing a duet. *That* was music? Of course, with Christmas coming, everybody needed the ten-dollar prize.

Butch couldn't even play triangle in second-grade music class, so she knew he wouldn't be in the contest. Thinking of Butch reminded her of Manuel.

What under the sun does he play? Suki said to herself. *I wish I knew. Well, one thing I do know—he won't be playing Bach on the piano! I'm the only one at the Louisa May Alcott School who can do that, though I'm just in fourth grade.*

Again, Suki played the bass notes in the last four measures of the piece, then repeated them with the other three parts, still louder than before. *Some climax,* she decided. *I can hear the applause. I'll slip off the piano bench and bow. If they keep on clapping, I'll curtsy. That's the way it was at the school contest. I hope it will be that way tomorrow night. I can see that prize check with my name on it—pay to the order of Suki Gosho.*

She was still practicing her bows when Daddy called, "If you've finished, Suki, please come down here and help me in the shop."

Every Saturday she hung the CLOSED sign in the shop's glass door and helped Daddy arrange a new display in the big front window for the Sunday strollers who stopped to look. Last of all, when he had finished counting the money in the cash drawer, he let her bag and stack it in the squatty corner safe. While he swept the floor with the broom, she emptied wastebaskets. That was when they talked if Daddy wasn't too tired. It was always very quiet by the time he locked the Clark Street door.

Tonight he said, "Let's get a breath of air. The last time I checked, the fattest snowflakes were coming down." They went outside. The sky was all silvery gauze . . . city lights blurred and floated through the swirling snow.

Suki threw back her head, shut her eyes, and stuck out her tongue. The frosty crystals melted on her tongue quicker than a wink. Street noises were muffled and the sidewalk was perfectly white except for the tracks of a stray dog, sniffing around the corner street light, his fur collar rumpled by the wind off the lake. *Could he feel the snow on his tongue?*

Snowflakes turned to drops of water on Daddy's glasses. It wasn't very cold yet, but he said, "Don't you get chilled." He put his arm around Suki. They stood there in the doorway, the shop lights casting two friendly shadows on the snow. Why, they were ten feet tall!

6

"*Ohayo gozaimasu,*" Mother chirped.

Why can't she say good morning in English, Suki wondered sleepily. *Reminds me of Manuel and those mysterious Spanish phrases he rattles off—he knows I don't know what they mean.*

"Here's a cup of tea to wake you, Suki."

"Tea? This early?"

"Asa-cha."

"Why?"

"Because your father wants you to see the snow that fell during the night before it gets all dirty. As soon as you're dressed, we'll walk through the park and have breakfast at Goshorn's Delicatessen on the way back. Don't dawdle."

The tea was steamy green in the white earthenware cup—the cup with a single branch of pussy willow painted on the inside. Now she remembered. It was an ancient Japanese custom to serve early morning tea on a winter day so that one could go outside in time to see the fresh fallen snow. Daddy had told her about doing that when he was a small boy.

> If we wait for dawn tomorrow,
> It may melt away, to our sorrow.

That was a line from a snow poem Daddy knew. *I'm glad he doesn't make me get up early every time it*

snows, Suki thought. *Going out will be fun though.* She finished the tea and dressed quickly. "I'm coming!" she yelled to Mother. Daddy and Mari and Yuri were already downstairs. She could hear their boots clumping across the bare floor of the shop.

Nothing happened during the walk. As usual, her sisters ran ahead, whispering and giggling and waving when there was no one to wave back.

"Visibility zero," Daddy remarked. "More snow on the way."

The fields and slopes of Lincoln Park were white. The snow made them seem bigger and empty. Overhead, blackbirds swooped and fussed. On the paths, pigeons and squirrels made dainty tracks. Suki had brought peanuts for them. Only the foxes were playing in the outside zoo cages.

"Look, Mother, at the snowflake I've caught," Suki said. "Isn't it perfect?"

"Yes, dear, it's perfect. Just think, there will never, never be another one like it."

The star design vanished, leaving no trace on Suki's woolly glove.

"Snowflakes and people—no two alike," Daddy said. "Why can't we appreciate our differences?"

With that question, a memory popped into Suki's head. Because Suki was *Nisei*—Japanese American—Butch and his gang had called her "Slant Eyes." Before she and Butch had got together, her best friend had been an invisible peacock. Best Friend, the Peacock, had explained to her that some people act as though differences are more important than being friends, because they haven't learned better. That was a long time ago. Butch doesn't act that way anymore, Suki thought. He's changed. He's my best pal since I outgrew that invisible peacock.

"Mother, may I ask Butch to go with us to the program tonight?"

"Of course, Suki. Butch is like one of the family."

Breakfast at Goshorn's . . . Sunday school at the Koinonia Koffee House . . . practice . . . pancakes for lunch . . . It was after one o'clock when Suki thought again about inviting Butch. She'd better give him a call.

When he answered the phone, she said, "Butch, this is Suki."

"Suki who? I thought it was Peppermint Patty."

"Idiot! Be serious. How about going with us to the program?"

There was a long pause. "That would be neat, but you see it's like this—I promised Manuel. His folks aren't going, so he's countin' on me to be his fan club. He's in the contest."

"Oh," Suki said flatly. "What's *he* going to do?"

"I don't know. He didn't tell me, honest, but we'll see you there, Suki. Okay?"

"Maybe I'll see you, maybe I won't." Suki slammed down the receiver. Bang.

7

Halfway through the Bach arrangement, Suki almost forgot the music, because, glancing up from the piano keyboard, she saw Manuel waiting his turn behind the stage curtain. Was he going to follow her on the program? He wasn't holding an instrument, and she knew he didn't play piano. What was he up to?

Just in the nick of time, the next measure came to Suki, and she played the rest of the piece with extra feeling. The final E-flat octave in the left hand was the loudest yet, and she held the pedal for what seemed a long, long time. Then the applause began—she was bowing, bowing, bowing—they liked her solo!

She even smiled a little at Manuel as she passed him backstage. Now she would find out what he was going to do. One thing Suki knew—there had been more applause for her piano solo than for her sisters' duet. Far more.

She no sooner found her seat in the front row of contestants than the director of the community programs said, "Manuel Arboleda will announce his own number."

At least he's combed his hair, Suki thought, as Manuel walked to the center of the small stage.

"*Buenas noches,*" Manuel said, smiling at the room full of people as though they were all old friends. "When I was a leetle baby, my grandmother rocked me to sleep, and the songs she sang to me were the same ones her grandmother sang to her when she was a leetle baby. Here is one I, Manuel Arboleda, want to geev to you—it always makes me feel safe."

Los pollitos dicen
pio, pio, pio
cuando tienen hambre
cuando tienen frio;
La gallina acude
y les presta abrigo
y hasta el otry dia
duermen los pollitos.

There was silence for a moment after Manuel finished, the silence one feels when under a spell, for the young clear voice had cast a spell over the listeners with its gaiety and tenderness.

In spite of herself, Suki knew that Manuel had really *given* all of them the song, as he said, and it was something very special which had belonged to him and to his ancestors. It made her think of last summer's vacation on St. Simons Island—of the friends she had made there, Renee and Cherry. They had *given* her a song, too.

Manuel was saying, "In English, the song goes like this."

The chicks say
pio, pio, pio
when they are hungry,
when they are cold;
The mother hen hurries
and puts them under her wings,
and until the next day
the chicks sleep.

Again there was that moment of magic silence when Manuel stopped singing. But it did not last. The clapping began and went on . . . and on . . . and on. . . .

Above the noise, some of the grown-ups called, "More! More! Sing it once more!"

Pleased, Manuel grinned, nodded, and motioned for quiet. He sang a second time in Spanish, and before the last note was finished, deafening applause burst all around. There was no doubt about who had won the contest. Suki knew the audience liked Manuel Arboleda's simple folk tune better than anything else on the program.

8

When Suki went to bed that night, it was late. Refreshments had been served at the Koffee House after the contest. Mr. and Mrs. Gosho had talked to some of the neighbors, but Suki had sat by herself until Butch and Manuel found her. She had tried to be nice to Manuel then, not that she could bring herself to say she was glad he had won. Instead, she had asked, "How are you going to spend your prize money?"

"Oh, I am going to enroll in the Telescope Makers class at the planetarium," Manuel had replied.

"Don't they have a long waiting list?"

"Sure, but Beeg Boy weel talk them into putting

hees name on top. You weel see." Suki knew he wasn't joking—he meant to be on top of the list. She might have said something nasty at that moment if the director hadn't interrupted to ask Manuel if he would sing regularly on the nights the Spanish-speaking kids came to the Koffee House. He had told Manuel, "You can take up a collection."

"At first they weel geev me dimes . . . then quarters . . . then dollars," Manuel had said, laughing. "Manuel weel—how do you say—put the Koffee House on the map."

That was when Daddy had called to her, "Time to go home, Suki." *What a relief!*

Now, Daddy was turning off lights, coming down the hall. She hoped he would go on by. She didn't want to talk. She only wanted to bury her face in the pillow and have a good cry.

"Asleep, Suki?"

Why did he ask when he knew better? She pretended to yawn.

"Almost."

Daddy came in and sat on the foot of her bed. He often did that.

"You played very well, Suki. We are proud of you."

"How could you be? I didn't win."

"Well, you can't win every time. You won the piano contest at school. After all, that one was tougher. Winning is fun, but it isn't all that matters by a long shot."

"I know that, Daddy, but the contest was so unfair!"

"Unfair? I'm afraid I don't know what you mean, Suki. The director explained that the winner would be the one who received the most applause. Don't you agree—Manuel did get the most?"

"Yes, but all he did was get up there and flash his big smile and sing that little old baby song. I practiced and practiced. Bach's hard!"

"That's true, my honey, but the contest wasn't to see who could do the most difficult thing. You did your best. That's more important than winning." Daddy sighed as he stood up.

"But why did it have to be *Manuel*?" Suki wailed.

Daddy leaned down and patted her cheek. "Next time, maybe you'll be the winner. 'Night."

9

I've turned over a trillion times, Suki complained to the dark.

She had tried everything—praying and counting sheep; even remembering those days last summer when the air had been hushed, the ocean smooth—nothing helped. She was wide awake, and questions kept piling one on top of the other, questions mostly about Manuel.

Why don't I like him? Is it because he brags all the time and acts so cocky? I bragged, too, when I won the other contest.

Is it because everyone (but me) likes him? They like me, too. They applauded my solo, too. He never cares how he looks . . . but Mother said I looked like a beach bum last summer while we were on the Island.

Is it his Spanish which Manuel knows I can't understand? And that accent which gets worse when he's excited? . . . But then, I use Japanese words sometimes when Butch makes me mad.

Is it the way Manuel laughs about everything? The janitor at school, Mr. Mainz, says I make him happy by smiling and laughing.

Is it because Manuel knows all about telescopes? I do wish I knew how to make one! But why does that bother me? I can go to the planetarium anytime and look at the whole sky, can't I? That's more fun than looking at stars one by one through an old homemade telescope . . . a homemade telescope . . . a homemade . . . a homemadetelescope . . . hommmmmtelessss . . . zeizzzz

. . . I must be dreaming . . . I'm asleep . . . I'm dreaming, that's why I can't get this Zeiss to focus! This telescope is even bigger than the one at the planetarium. Maybe if I turn these dials I can clear things up. . . . There, that's better. I can scan space as easily as looking out a window. Whee!

What's that . . . coming right toward me? A star? Yes, yes, it's a star, and it's exploding fountains of light . . . white changing to yellow and blue and red . . . all the colors of the rainbow shooting in every direction!

The star was traveling so fast now, the colors trailed behind . . . it was expanding, expanding, coming nearer, rushing waves of sound at Suki . . .

sound that pulsed like intermingling cymbals and music boxes and choirs and waterfalls and castanets and sirens . . . closer . . . closer . . . closer until Suki heard the planetarium lecturer say in an echoing voice, “The Star of Bethlehem!”

The sound stopped.

So did the star—close to her, shimmering and golden. And right in the very heart of it was a figure, a figure Suki could barely see. She adjusted the dials on her giant telescope to magnify the figure until it was as large as a man.

It was a man. He was resting under a leafy tree and on His right shoulder perched a peacock, its coppery train sweeping the ground, its breast glistening blue and green.

"Best Friend!" Suki cried, but the Peacock did not seem to hear her.

Then she noticed that the Man had an arm around a boy who stood at His other side.

"Manuel!" Suki called, but Manuel did not see her. He was looking at the Man, who all of a sudden held out His hands and said, "Come to me."

Three people walked single file toward Him. They knelt and placed brightly wrapped presents at His feet.

"Why, that's Mr. Mainz, the school janitor," Suki gasped. "And Renee from St. Simons Island, and Butch!"

"Shh," the lecturer warned. "The Man on the star is speaking."

The voice was gentle but strong as was the Man's face. "You Magi have come a long way," He said.

"We followed your star," Butch said.

"Are you really Immanuel?" asked Mr. Mainz.

"Yes, I am Immanuel." The Man smiled at the Spanish boy beside Him. "I am God with you."

"With us here on the star or in *our* world?" Renee asked.

"On all stars, in all worlds," the Man answered. "I am with you always."

"But I have never seen you anywhere before!" Renee exclaimed to the Man.

"Renee, some things are real even though you can't see them."

Renee took one of His hands in hers to make sure He was real. There was a deep scar in the palm. "I love you," she said.

"That's because I loved you first." The Man smiled again and kept speaking. "My love is a gift you can share with everyone. When you get back home, do that. *Do that.*"

The Magi with the familiar faces of Mr. Mainz and Renee and Butch turned around and walked slowly away from the Man, right toward Suki.

"I must go where my friends are, to the *wonder star*," Suki said to the lecturer.

"Oh, but you can't. It's too late," he said. "Christmas is over."

The star began moving . . . away from her . . . swiftly drifting . . . drifting . . . drifting through the vibrating, tremulous colors into a giant spiral of stars . . . a vast galaxy of stars. . . .

Soon she could not tell it from the others, but the wonder of it did not go away.

10

Haunted by the strange and beautiful dream, Suki awakened early the next morning. Once she was fully conscious, she knew the planetarium lecturer had been wrong. Christmas wasn't over. It hadn't come yet.

Seeing Manuel in the dream, so close to Jesus, must have meant something, something she should be able to figure out for herself. Christmas was Jesus' birthday, and she kept hearing Him say, "My love is a gift you can share with everyone." *That included Manuel. He loves Manuel and me and Butch and Renee and Mr. Mainz . . . everyone!* "My love is a gift . . . my love is a gift you can share. . . ."

It wasn't too late. There were still six days to shop. *I know what I'll do. When I bought the nutmeg brown turtleneck shirt to give Butch, I knew Manuel was the one who needed it. But I didn't want to give that big show-off anything then. This morning I do! If he enrolls in the Telescope Makers class at the planetarium, the first thing he'll need is a mirror for his scope.*

If I can afford it, I'll give Manuel the mirror.

At breakfast, Suki said, "Daddy, I have one more present to buy."

Daddy was hidden behind the morning paper. "Well, school will be out Thursday. After that we can go downtown again. Will that be soon enough?"

"I guess, but Butch is coming over for his present Thursday. I'd like to have this other thing ready then."

"Is 'this other thing' a big secret?" Daddy asked. "Because I may go to the Loop as soon as I get the lights on the tree. That is, if your mother will watch the shop."

"That's a sneaky way to ask me," Mother said. Her voice sounded cross, but as she took Daddy's cereal bowl, she kissed the top of his head, and while she put the oatmeal pan to soak, she hummed "Deck the Hall with Boughs of Holly."

Suki wanted to tell them her plan, but how could she? They knew very well how she had treated Manuel, how she had tried to make him feel shut out.

Before Manuel had moved into the neighborhood, Butch had liked Suki best. She couldn't be sure of that anymore.

Lately, a lump of fear almost choked her. It made her want to keep Butch all for herself, to be smarter

than Manuel about telescopes and stars and space, to win every contest.

Last night the lump had hurt more than ever before, and her parents knew how mean she had been. But this morning she didn't feel mean or furious or hurt. Something was changing deep inside her, and it had to do with what Jesus said about His love being a gift, a gift that could be shared.

She sat up very straight. "If I have enough money left in my Christmas Club account, I want to buy a mirror for Manuel."

Daddy peered over the *Tribune*, surprised.

Mother looked surprised, too. "A mirror? Do boys look at themselves these days?"

"Not that kind of mirror," Suki said. "The kind the kids grind at the Telescope Makers shop."

"At the Adler Planetarium?"

"Yes. You see, Manuel is going to use his prize money to enroll in the class, but that costs ten dollars," Suki explained. "He won't have anything left for the mirror."

"How will he pay for the other parts then?" Daddy asked.

"Oh, the Koffee House director wants him to sing regularly. Manuel can take up a collection each time. He'll save."

"Very interesting," Daddy said. "Well, I guess I could go on to the planetarium from my appointment and pick up that mirror for you. Hadn't you better find out how much it costs? You may not have enough money."

What a dreadful thought. But the woman who answered the planetarium phone when Suki called said there were two telescope kits. The smaller one required a four-and-a-quarter-inch mirror blank.

"How much does that one cost?" Suki asked.

"Six dollars," the woman answered.

Six dollars was a lot of money to spend on a present, especially for someone outside the family—someone she hadn't even allowed to be her friend.

11

Finally it was Thursday.

Suki was so excited she acted silly. When she had asked Manuel to come to her house with Butch after school, he had seemed almost scared. Butch, too. Would they ever be surprised!

In the shop closet, Daddy found a wooden box the right size for the mirror, its excelsior packing still inside. Suki watched as he carefully wrapped the mirror in white tissue paper, then nestled it in the shreds of fragrant wood. Mother suggested tying green yarn on the box rather than covering it with Christmas paper. They used the same yarn on Butch's package. Suki placed the two gifts under the tree in the family room.

The boys were to be there by four o'clock. Suki was dying of suspense. *It was almost five, why didn't those dumb-dumbs come on?*

Nervous and stuttering, Butch and Manuel finally arrived. Suki was nervous, too, so nervous she said, "Good morning."

"*Ella es muy tonta* [She is stupid]," Manuel whispered to Butch.

To Suki he said, "Good morning, but isn't it afternoon, or are we early?" Suki and Butch giggled. While she hung up their coats, they inspected the tree.

"Looks like a Mexican tree with all the poppies and birds," Manuel said. "Beeeeeeautiful."

"It's Japanese," Suki said. "And those aren't poppies, they're anemones. My sisters made them."

"Poppies or whatever, it's sure pretty," Butch said.

"I made something for you, Suki." Manuel handed her a red tin box. "Remember the day I said sweets are for leetle children?" He laughed. "This we call *dulce de leche* [sweet of milk] a sort of fudge. I make eet so good, my mother sells eet."

He's bragging just for fun, Suki realized for the first time. *And I don't mind Manuel teasing me for being "leetle."* She snapped open the lid on the red tin box and popped a whole piece of the sweet into her mouth. "Brazil nuts and cinnamon!" she shrieked, rolling her eyes crazily.

"You can't eat my present, Suki," Butch said, handing her a thin square-shaped gift.

"I'll bet I can guess, Butch."

"What?"

"A record."

"Yeah, but what?"

Suki ripped off the wrapping. "*Snoopy vs. the Red Baron*! Oh, Butch, how did you know I wanted that? Thanks. We'll play it as soon as you guys open your gifts."

She picked up their packages under the tree and handed the flat one to Butch. The wooden box tied with green yarn she handed to Manuel.

In no time, Butch was holding up his new shirt. "Manuel, take a look at this—a turtleneck!"

Manuel did not even glance at the shirt. He was lifting a mysterious object from a nest of excelsior. Ever so slowly he removed the tissue around it until the plain disc of glass lay cradled in his hands. From the expression on his face, it might have been a diamond. A telescope mirror . . . his own telescope mirror to grind and polish and fit . . . his at last.

Suki waited for him to say something, but for once Manuel was speechless.

"That's just the size you wanted," Butch said. Still, Manuel could not speak. Suki began to wonder if the mirror had been a mistake. Could he have changed his mind about building a telescope? Then

she saw that Manuel was blinking—blinking to keep back tears in his dark eyes.

"You weel not believe this, but I cry when I am happy. Excuse me." Manuel sniffled and wiped at his nose. The next instant he was smiling again. "With thees mirror, Beeg Boy weel build the best telescope in all the world—the very best!" he said, waving his arms. "And eef you leetle keeds are good, I weel let you look at the stars through eet. I weel first grind eet rough. Then I weel grind eet fine. I weel polish. I weel test. I weel coat eet with four millionth of an inch of aluminum film. Four millionth of an inch! Eet weel be that exact. Eet weel be perfect. Eet weel be the best telescope in all the world—the very best!"

"Suki, we're going to have to listen to that from now until the 'best telescope in all the world' is finished." Butch grinned.

"Good grief," Suki cried, holding her head. "I hope not!" The three of them laughed; then they were all talking at once.

Suki had forgotten to shut Manuel out. He was her friend the same as Butch. He even seemed like "one of the family" the way Butch did.

Now, she understood about the dream—about the Man on the wonder star who had said, "My love is a gift you can share with everyone."

Only by sharing His love could you be *with* another person as she was *with* Manuel now.

Christmas would never be over.

God is with us—always.

Dulce de Leche [sweet of milk]

1 quart milk
1 1/2 cups sugar
1/2 teaspoon vanilla

Combine milk and sugar in saucepan. Heat to boiling. Stirring constantly, reduce heat until mixture bubbles steadily. Cook for two hours or until sauce or pudding or fudge consistency is reached. (Stir occasionally.) When it is as thick as you wish, remove from heat. Add vanilla.

This recipe is for six servings as sauce; four servings as pudding.

Latin-Americans use *dulce de leche* as a sauce poured over fresh or canned fruit, cake, pudding, or ice cream. As Manuel's fudge, cook until it thickens and add chopped brazil nuts and some cinnamon.

—From the author's friends, the Meneses

Joyce Blackburn has written fifteen published books since leaving a professional career in Chicago radio. Her recording of *Suki and the Invisible Peacock* led to a contract for her first book of the same title. Subsequent prize-winning titles for young readers have made Blackburn well-known among librarians and teachers. She has also gained recognition in the field of popular historical biography and enjoys an enthusiastic adult following. Blackburn, a resident of St. Simons Island, Georgia, received the 1996 Governor's Award in the humanities from the Georgia Humanities Council. Her works are in the Special Collections of the Woodruff Library at Emory University, Atlanta, Georgia.